YOU'RE IN THE SADDLE, PARDNER.

Chasing a band of dangerous kidnappers ...
Starring in a cowboy movie ...
Rescuing the president ...
Playing drums for a pop music group ...

What happens in this book is up to you, according to the choices you make, page by page. You'll find over thirty possible endings, from scary to silly to surprising. And it all starts with your choice of a campsite....

Ask for these other Making Choices books:

THE CEREAL BOX ADVENTURES, by Barbara
    Bartholomew
FLIGHT INTO THE UNKNOWN, by Barbara
    Bartholomew
PROFESSOR Q'S MYSTERIOUS MACHINE, by Donna
    Fletcher Crow

THE PRESIDENT'S STUCK IN THE MUD
AND OTHER WILD WEST ESCAPADES

STEPHEN A. BLY

Chariot Books

**For Dervy
and the guys**

First printing, September 1982
Third printing, January 1985

THE PRESIDENT'S STUCK IN THE MUD and Other Wild West
Escapades
© 1982 Stephen A. Bly for text and Scott Gustafson for
illustrations.
Book and series design by Ray Cioni/The Cioni Artworks.

ISBN: 0-89191-661-X
LC: 82-71337

CAUTION!

This is not a normal book! If you read it straight through, it won't make sense.

Instead, you must start at page 1 and then turn to the pages where your choices lead you. Your first situation—choosing a campsite during a family vacation—is one you might make anytime. But after that, your decisions can lead you into crazy and dangerous places—and even to a world you never knew existed.

If you want to read this book, you must choose to
Turn to page 1.

It took three hard days of driving to get here. Hours of staring at highway signs, hundreds of miles of spelling your name with the letters on billboards— and six states of constant griping by your twin sisters. They may be older than you, but they aren't exactly mature, in your opinion.

Finally, here you all are at Yellowstone National Park, Wyoming, but still they argue. It seems they can't agree on which campground to stay at. All you want to do is get out and explore. But, no, first you have to spend an hour touring every camp- site from Mammoth Hot Springs to Norris.

Carrie wants to stay at Indian Creek Camp- ground. She says it has lots of room. Cherrie is pouting, holding out for Ponderosa Overlook.

You know the real reason Cherrie wants to go to Ponderosa is because she saw some cute boys up there. You saw something the others missed— a deluxe travel home with California plates, and a silver monogrammed "Buck" above the front grill. Could it be him?

On the other hand, Indian Creek Campground must have a nice creek somewhere.

As usual, your dad has to turn to you. "Looks like the twins can't make up their minds. Which camp- ground shall we stay at?"

Choices: You choose Ponderosa Overlook (turn to page 3).
You choose Indian Creek (turn to page 2).

2

You pick out a really good campsite close to the creek. Cherrie is mad at you. She's claiming that her sinuses are already plugged up. But you stay out of her way and jump right in to help your dad set up camp.

With all the gear in place, plenty of water hauled up for mom, and your hiking boots on, you grab your Polaroid camera and head to the creek for some excitement.

"Stay close to the creek so you don't get lost," dad yells.

"We wouldn't want to have to come find you," one of the twins giggles.

"Boy, that'll be the day," you mumble under your breath.

Two signs catch your eye as you approach fast-moving Dryers Creek. Down the creek, along the trail, is a sign. "Caution: Dangerous Bear Area. Proceed at your own risk."

Looking up the creek you notice an old, broken sign with a mysterious message: "4.5 Miles to Hidden ...." (The rest of the sign is broken off.)

"Hidden what?" you wonder.

Choices: **You head downstream, even though there is a bear warning (turn to page 4).**
You start hiking upstream to discover what is "hidden" (turn to page 7).

You kick a pinecone across the gravel drive as you walk around the loop at Ponderosa Overlook campground. Your dad instructed you to find the best site while he stopped to talk to the ranger.

"Number 23's not too bad," you say to yourself. It's large enough, and located halfway between the water and the outhouses.

You notice that next door, in site 22, are three large tents crowded into one little clearing. Then you notice a man carrying some drum cases into the green tent. Your drum set at home has similar cases, but these drums are Ludwigs. The best.

You are hurrying back to dad to suggest site 23 when you notice the travel home you saw earlier. It's a Golden Ranchero Deluxe. You notice again the California plates, plus a Beverly Hills license frame and the silver "Buck" above the grill. "Could it really be him?" you wonder again.

Next to the travel home is empty site #14.

Choices: You pick site 23 (turn to page 6).
You pick site 14 (turn to page 5).

Hiking downhill is easier than uphill, but you worry about the bear sign. You start to whistle.

The cold, sparkling water reminds you that you meant to bring your canteen as well as the camera. Now you're thirsty, but you're determined not to go back to camp. You can get a drink out of the creek.

As you bend down to scoop some ice-cold refreshment, you notice two things. First, out in the middle of the stream is a container with a mirror-like surface, reflecting the noonday sun. It's about the size of a fruitcake box, but you can't tell what it is.

The other distraction is right here in the mud next to your knee. It's a human footprint, one of several. You're surprised not only at the fact that someone is going barefoot out in the woods, but also that at the unbelievably large foot. You wear size 9 shoes, and you can put your two boots end-to-end into one of these tracks.

Choices: You follow the gigantic tracks away from the stream (turn to page 11). You decide to retrieve the tin box in the middle of the stream (turn to page 25).

As soon as camp is set up, the twins get into another argument about who should stay in camp and wait for Uncle Bill and family, and who should go with your mom and dad into the town of West Yellowstone for supplies.

Your dad tells them they'll have to stay together until they stop arguing. So then he turns to you and gives you the option.

Choices: **You stay in camp and let the twins go to town (turn to page 15).**
You go to West Yellowstone and the twins stay in camp (turn to page 8).

You spend the next hour setting up camp and keeping one eye on the tents next door. During that time you notice that all the campers seem to be in their late teens or early twenties. Besides the drum set, you notice other instruments being carried into the green tent. Your curiosity is building. Finally, camp is complete. You mom and dad and the twins head off to town for groceries.

All you have to do is take the money envelopes down to the ranger station, and then wait in camp for your Uncle Bill, Aunt Judy, and cousins Scott and Stephen to show up. They're on their way up from California to spend this vacation with you.

You notice one of the girls struggling to carry a guitar amplifier from the van to the green tent. You could offer to help. Maybe it would be a way to get to know them.

Just then your dad's parting words ring in your ears. "Get up to that ranger station right away. If we don't hurry and pay the fee for both spaces, Uncle Bill and Aunt Judy won't have a place to camp."

Choices: You postpone the trip to the ranger station and help the girl with the amp (turn to page 12).
You hurry to the ranger station, hoping to get back and introduce yourself to your neighbors (turn to page 18).

"Well, whatever is hidden is really hidden," you say to yourself as the trail seemingly ends at a marshy swamp next to the creek.

The marsh is beautiful. The grass is about a foot tall, and bright orange and blue wild flowers are sprinkled across it. But whenever you take a step, the water and mud come almost to the top of your hiking boots. You can see a slight trail across the meadow, but a swarm of mosquitoes thwarts your progress.

You notice that just upstream is an old log lying across the creek. At this point the creek is about two feet deep and extremely swift. The log is old, mossy, and shows signs that the tiny wood beetles have nearly finished their destroying work.

"Maybe it will hold me up if I go very slowly," you mutter.

Something "hidden" is up the trail a ways, and you are determined to find out what it is.

Choices: **You head through the marshy meadow of mosquitoes (turn to page 9).**
You take your chances on the old log (turn to page 10).

Your folks park the car in a supermarket parking lot. "Now be back here in an hour," they say. "We don't want to have to come looking for you."

You start to walk down the wooden sidewalk, past the tourist shops, and two sights catch your attention.

One is a poster describing a rare white buffalo that is on display at the West Yellowstone museum. The other is a real stagecoach hitched up to a lamppost over by the bank.

Choices: **You go over to the museum to see the white buffalo (turn to page 17).**
You decide to look more closely at the stagecoach (turn to page 43).

The marsh turns out to be more treacherous than you first thought. The mud in the middle is now well over your boots. You feel the sticky, black slime clinging to your socks, yet you trudge on.

Suddenly you begin to sink even further. The mud is up past your knees now, and the suction is so strong that you can't pull your leg out.

You're stuck!

The mosquitoes are diving at you like hungry diners' forks at the last pork chop. Frantically you look around for someone to help. There's no one in sight.

You begin to panic. "Dear God, please help me!" you cry. Mud now covers your arms from several useless attempts to free yourself.

Suddenly, off to the right, you notice movement among the small trees at the edge of the woods.

Perhaps it's dad? Even one of the twins would do.

But your hope evaporates when you get a view of what was making all the commotion.

Turn to page 29.

The log proved to be plenty strong. You have no problem crossing it. Then you tramp on up the creek. Along the way you see tracks of horses in the dusty trail. You wave to a man who's fishing along the opposite bank.

Up ahead, a small, deerlike animal crosses the trail. It runs like a little deer, but its head is different. "It's so ugly!" you comment to yourself.

You hurry up to try to get a picture of the animal. But just as you are close enough, something in the camera viewfinder catches your attention. There, tucked back in the pines, is an old log cabin.

As you straighten up to get a better view, you frighten the animal.

Choices: **You follow the little animal to get a good photo (turn to page 120).**
You go over and explore the cabin (turn to page 14).

Those oversized tracks soon depart from the trail. They lead you right up to a bluff where a little snowmelt stream falls off into the main part of Dryers Creek.

Looks like there are only two ways down. You can slide down a mossy granite rock about ten feet long and hope to stop before falling onto the rocks. Or you could jump off into the deep pool of water at the bottom of the miniature falls. It looks deep enough that you don't think you'd hurt yourself.

You almost decide to forget the whole thing and return to the trail when you notice that the big tracks follow the creek down below.

"Big tracks. Big feet. Bigfoot!" You are startled at your own thought. You'd heard in school about the western legend of a giant creature called Bigfoot or Sasquatch. You don't know whether to be scared or excited. But you are going to go on.

Choices: You slide down the mossy granite and take your chances with the rocks (turn to page 16).
You dive into the pool (turn to page 21).

"Hi, I'm Tina," the girl with the amplifier introduces herself. She accepts your offer of help. As you enter the tent, you see several musical instruments in place as if for a concert or practice for a concert.

"Hey," you ask, "are you guys a band? I mean, are you a pop group?"

"Sure!" Tina laughs. "This doesn't look like a Coleman stove, does it?"

"What are you called?" you ask excitedly. "Have I ever heard of you?"

"We're the Idaho Blue Mountain Stampede. Ever heard of us?" she asks.

"Er, no. Not really," you admit. "But then I'm not from around here."

"Well, nobody else has heard of us either," Tina says, "but things will change tomorrow night. You see, they're going to tape 'Musicscene' down at the lodge by Old Faithful tomorrow night. You know, a Fourth of July special. And we're on the show! It's our first time on national tv. We're really excited. But then it all depends on Russ."

"Russ?"

"Russ Stewart, drummer and lead singer," she replies as she continues to set up some equipment. "He hurt himself this morning."

Turn to page 19.

You enter the cabin thinking that it's just an abandoned relic, but inside you discover differently. It's old, and dusty, and messy, but someone lives in it. You can tell by the clothes, dishes, and food. A gigantic bearskin covers the bed, and on the wall is a large moose head.

"That's what that animal was," you exclaim to yourself. "A baby moose!"

You touch one of the biscuits in the frying pan that's sitting on a cold wood stove, and find it to be as hard as a rock. Whoever lives here has been gone quite a while.

Then you see it hanging on the post in the middle of the room: a map scribbled out on buckskin. From this side of the room all you can see is the title: "Gold Mine X."

You move closer to get a better look until something makes you freeze in your tracks. There, coiled around the center post and poised for attack, is a diamondback rattlesnake! Both of you are motionless, waiting for the other to make the first move.

Choices: You slowly try to reach for the map (turn to page 20).
You abandon the whole project and back out of the cabin (turn to page 27).

The first order of business, as far as you are concerned, is to find out who your neighbors really are. You look for an excuse. Finally, when a tall man leaves the travel home heading towards the ranger station, you make your move.

With camera in hand, you approach the man and say, "Aren't you Buck Slade, the movie star?"

"That's right, kid," he replies in his unmistakable drawl.

"Really? I mean, are you really THE Buck Slade?" you repeat.

"Well, last time I looked in the mirror I was," he replies.

You laugh, and continue to walk with him. "Say, Mr. Slade, could I take a picture of you?"

"Well, I'd rather that you didn't. See, my agent likes to control all the photos that are taken. That way we have some say over ones that don't turn out so good. But listen, if you'll run this pay envelope down to the ranger for me, I'll get you one out of the travel home."

You quickly agree.

Turn to page 24.

Sliding was a worse idea than you thought. Unable to keep your balance, you tumble head over heels into the rocks below. Trying to brace your fall, you stiffen your legs—and catch your right ankle on the top of a sharp boulder.

You struggle to get to your feet. The pain is unbearable. There's no choice now; you have to try to get back to camp.

You crawl over to the edge of the brush and find a stick to use as a crutch. That's when you discover there was another way down the bluff. An almost hidden trail leads back uphill and towards camp.

You stop at the original sighting of the tracks to take a picture. Phooey. Your camera was damaged in the fall!

Back in camp, dad loads you into the car for the drive up to the hospital at Mammoth Hot Springs. You start to tell him about the metal box in the creek, and suddenly Carrie interrupts. "Yeah, wait till you hear the big story about seeing a monster," she sneers.

"Oh?" your dad says curiously.

"Yes." You speak in a very loud voice so that both twins will hear. "And the tracks were headed right back here toward camp!"

Carrie turns pale.

"What's the matter, sis?" you ask with a smile. "I thought you didn't believe in monsters."

THE END

A sign at the corner points toward the museum. You cross the busy highway and head for the building you believe houses the white buffalo. Suddenly, from behind a clump of pines, an Indian boy about your age appears. He's riding a large pinto horse, has long black hair, and is dressed in buckskin. In his hand is a long spear decorated with yellow and red feathers.

He yells, "Where are you going, paleface?" and points the spear right at you.

Choices: You holler back, "Get out of my way or I'll call the cavalry!" (turn to page 37).

You explain that you were merely looking for the museum so you could see the white buffalo (turn to page 53).

A sign at the ranger station diverts your attention from any other thoughts. "The president of the United States will tour the park at approximately 2:00 P.M. today." As the ranger takes your money, he tells you the president will be by any moment now. He's about to close up shop and go out to the highway himself.

You run all the way back to the camp to get your Polaroid camera. By the time you reach the highway, it's crowded with onlookers.

Choices: **You stand in the crowd and hope to slip in front of others to get a good photo (turn to page 22).**
You climb the hill behind the road for a better viewing spot (turn to page 26).

"You need a drummer?" you exclaim.

"Yeah. Say, do you know—" Tina stops as a young, bushy-haired man enters the tent. Later you find out he is Mike Stephens, their lead guitar player.

"Bad news. It's a real bummer," he announces. The others in the tent stop and listen.

"The doc up at Mammoth says Russ has a compound fracture in his arm. Insisted that he go up to the hospital to have it set. There's no way he's going to play any drums for six weeks."

"But he'll miss the concert!" a girl named Joyce replies.

"That's a fact," Mike states.

Joyce groans. "What happens now? This is our once-in-a-lifetime chance! Where's Russ now?"

"Valerie drove him up to the hospital in Billings," Mike says. "Now, as far as the concert is concerned, I figure Tina and I can sing the leads if we have to. But where in all Wyoming will we find a drummer at the last minute?"

Choices: You mention to Tina that you can play the drums (turn to page 40). You tell Mike you noticed that The Waco Brothers are in Jackson, and suggest their drummer to fill in (turn to page 36).

Slowly you reach for the buckskin. The snake doesn't even flinch but stays ready to attack. You are about to chicken out when all of a sudden your feet trip and you fall straight towards the deadly snake.

Turn to page 23.

Somewhere in midair, an awful thought hits you. Your camera will get wet! You hold it high in the air as you sink into the frigid creek water.

"Hey, kid, you always swim with all your clothes on?" several older boys shout from the creek bank. Crawling out of the water with a partially dry Polaroid, you blush at the way you must look to them. "Didn't you know there was a trail over by the bushes?"

You feel like a fool. The boys continue their trek back to camp, and you go on downstream, not telling them about the tracks you are following.

"What dorks. They didn't even see these tracks! They must be city kids," you mutter. Your four hours in Yellowstone have made you a seasoned westerner, at least in your mind.

Bam! A rock whizzes by your head and crashes against a large boulder next to the trail, interrupting your thoughts. Who threw …?

You look up. There in the brush about fifty yards ahead of you is a huge, hairy … man? Animal? It must be Bigfoot! You are partially hidden from the creature in the rocks along the creek, and you marvel that it could spot you so readily.

Rrrhhoar!

What's that? This sound is right above you on the big boulder. Another Bigfoot?

Turn to page 54.

It takes about half an hour before the black presidential car rounds the bend by the picnic tables and heads your way. You can hardly wait to see him. And you can hardly wait to tell the family about seeing the president. Carefully you crowd your way past an older couple, in between two giggling girls, and in front of some small children, just about the moment the president passes by.

"He looks younger than his pictures," you comment to the person next to you.

The president waves in your direction and you lift the camera with careful aim. **Snap!** A perfect picture of a waving, smiling U.S. president.

Perfect until the Polaroid film begins to develop. As you walk back to camp the picture becomes clear. You have a beautiful shot of the back of a little kid's hand waving.

"Oh, no!" you cry.

"Oh, yes," the twins reply later that night as you try to explain the messed-up photo.

"Really, I did see him. He waved right at me," you explain. "He's a lot younger looking than I thought."

"I should say," Carrie chimes in. "Look at how small his hand is!"

Everyone laughs.

Except you.

THE END

You are convinced you are dying, but you didn't feel a sting. Looking up, you notice the snake still in its original pose. It's not looking at you, but is blithely staring at the front door.

Then it dawns on you. "It's dead. It's a fake!" you exclaim to an empty cabin. Cautiously you approach the snake once more.

Turn to page 33.

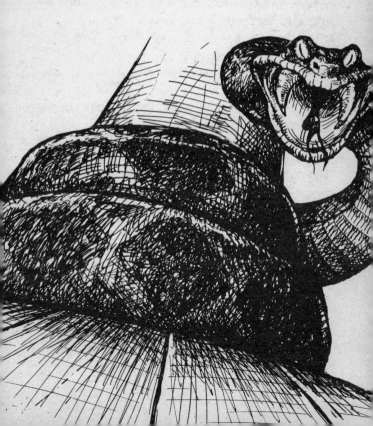

When you return to the travel home, Buck is sitting on the steps.

"Sorry, kid, I'm all out of photos," he says. "Listen, why don't you come on down to the set with me this afternoon? I've got plenty of photos down there. Have you ever seen a movie being filmed?"

"A movie?" you reply. "You mean you're making a movie here?"

"That's right, just over that draw up yonder. A whole movie set. Can't see a thing from here, though. That's just the way we want it. Too many gawkers slow the production time. We're making 'High Mountain Revenge.'"

"Really? Why, I've seen all of your movies. Sure I'd like to go!" you say.

"Well, go get your gear. I'm headin' up there right now," Buck states.

You run back to your tent, but can't for the life of you figure out what gear you are supposed to get. Finally you grab your sheepskin coat and your cowboy hat.

That's when you remember that you are supposed to wait in camp for your Uncle Bill and Aunt Judy to come along. You have to be there to show them their camping site.

Choices: **You tell Buck you can't go, and remain in camp (turn to page 30).**
You go with Buck and let your relatives fend for themselves (turn to page 32).

You find out there's a good reason for the tin box staying out in the middle of the stream; it won't budge at all. Even by wading out to it in the cold water, you can't seem to dig it up. You determine that you need a stick to pry it out with.

Looking along the bank you are unable to spot any kind of stick that is strong enough and straight enough. Then you spot the snow marker along the trail. You've been here in the winter months, so you know there is cross-country snow skiing in this region, and the trails are marked with eight-foot sticks painted bright red on the top.

The marker is perfect for your purposes. But try as you may, you can't pull it up to "borrow" it for a pry. The only way you can use the snow marker is to break it off.

Choices: **You break off the snow marker (turn to page 34).**
You return to the stream and try to dig out the box with your hands (turn to page 123).

You can see better from the top of the hill, all right, but you realize that you are too far away for a good picture.

Choices: **You return to the crowd to take your chances (turn to page 22).**
You try hiking down a little dirt road on the back side of the hill, hoping it leads you to a better view (turn to page 31).

You are somewhat surprised that the snake never moves a muscle as you back away toward the door. Once outside, you heave a deep sigh of relief and head back to the creek.

Then something you learned in science class dawns on you. Diamondbacks seldom are found as high as four thousand feet above sea level, you remember. Yellowstone Park is at an elevation of six thousand feet. What's going on?

Cautiously you reenter the cabin and proceed toward the motionless snake.

Turn to page 33.

Waddling out of the woods in a poky, unhurried manner is a huge beaver. "Wow! It must be two feet tall and four feet long," you exclaim to yourself. "But, Lord, I had in mind better help than a dumb animal."

Both the Lord and the animal ignore you.

Slowly surveying your condition, the big beaver lazily heads back for the little stand of aspen trees by the woods. For several minutes you hear a funny grinding sound coming from the aspen grove. Then, without warning, the tallest tree comes crashing down right towards you!

You duck to one side, and the tree misses you by inches. For a minute you thought you were a goner.

"Stupid beaver!" you yell out to no one in particular. Then it dawns on you. You'll be able to grab the aspen branches and pull yourself out of the mud. As you do, you can't help thinking that the beaver did it on purpose.

Finally you reach dry ground. You make up your mind to hike up through the woods, around the marsh, and back to the creek. There you can clean up and start over on your search, this time using the log crossing.

Just then the weirdest thing you have ever seen takes place.

Turn to page 39.

That night around the campfire you tell the whole gang about meeting Buck Slade.

Cherrie just laughs. "Yeah," she says, "and I met Chief Sitting Bull."

"Really, I did," you protest.

"Oh, sure," your cousin Stephen protests.

"Really!" a voice from the shadows replies.

Everyone jumps and turns to see the tall movie star walk toward the fire, carrying some pictures in one hand and a guitar in the other.

The whole family is staring, mouths open, as Buck enters the circle and hands you several pictures.

"Here are those pictures I promised. Old Buck never goes back on a promise. Code of the West, you know. Say, little buddy, mind if I sit in on the campfire and pick a song or two?" he asks you.

"Of course not. Here, Buck, sit over here." You motion to a log.

"Say, aren't you going to introduce me to these pretty twins?" Buck asks.

"Not me," you say with a smile. "They think you are a figment of my imagination."

Everyone laughs. Except the twins.

THE END

You haven't traveled one hundred feet before there is a chain across the road and a sign marked, "Park Service Road: No Admittance."

Choices: **You ignore the sign, climb over the chain, and continue (turn to page 38).**
You turn around and hike down the road in the opposite direction (turn to page 69).

As soon as you crest the hill in Buck's pickup truck, you can see the whole movie set sprawled across the canyon. People are scurrying in every direction. Buck gets you a tag to wear that allows you to be on the set. Then he hands you a guest ticket.

"This will get you some chuck." He points toward a large semitrailer parked at one end of the canyon.

"Chuck?" you echo.

"Lunch. It's a catering service. Just give them this pass and you can have anything you want. Now, if you want to see some action, sit up by that little red fir and just watch. I'm due in makeup," Buck says.

You nod and watch him hike up to a trailer with a big silver star on it. After a few minutes of looking around and trying to stay out of the way, you hike over to the little fir tree and sit down.

An hour later there has still been no action, and Buck hasn't come out of the trailer.

Choices: You wait a while longer for some action (turn to page 60).
You head down toward the catering service to get some lunch (turn to page 52).

You are right! The snake's a phony. It is a real rattlesnake, but it's dead and has been stuffed to look as if it was about to attack. What a sight! You think about taking it back to camp to scare your sisters, but notice that it was stuffed after it was coiled around the post. It would be almost impossible to remove.

The map is also fastened to the post. The old buckskin would surely crumble if you yanked on it.

Hurriedly you search the cabin for a pencil. There's none to be found. Finally you take a piece of wood ash from the stove, grab a short plank from the corner, and make your own copy of the map. As you leave the cabin, you try to make sure everything is just the way you found it.

Outside you look at the first instruction for finding the mine. "50 past red fir," it says. That's 50 steps, you assume. But which tree is the fir?

You try hard to remember the lecture the ranger at Yosemite gave last year when you were there. Had he said that pines have long needles in clusters of two and three? If so, this tree in the front yard must be a pine. Or is it a fir?

The tree in the back is pyramid-shaped, with even, single, short needles. "Maybe that one's the pine," you muse. "Why didn't I listen more closely to Ranger Doug last year?"

Choices: You choose the tree in front with long, clustered needles (turn to page 48). You call the one in back with short needles a fir (turn to page 61).

The stick proves harder to break than you thought. You pull and pull on the top, yet it holds. Finally you give it all you've got, and with a re-sounding **snap** the pole breaks off about a foot from the ground. You go tumbling backwards across the trail, holding on to the seven-foot re-mains.

"Hey, you! We're going to report you for de-stroying government property. What do you think you're doing?"

You look up from your spot on the ground and see three boys wearing football jerseys headed down the trail your way.

The biggest one comes over to you. You're still lying on the rocks. He repeats his question, "What are you doing?"

Choices: You decide to tell the guys about the tin box (turn to page 41).
You tell them you're making a splint for your injured ankle (turn to page 59).

Mike explodes with anger. "Who's this kid? Since when do we need advice from a stranger? The Waco Brothers. Nothing but scum!"

Tina pulls you aside as Mike continues to rant and rave. "Mike had a run-in with them last fall in Denver. Real bad blood, you know what I mean?"

For a moment you think about mentioning your ability to play the drums, but right then what you really want to do is get out of the tent. You could go reserve your Uncle Bill's campsite.

Choices: You mention that you play the drums (turn to page 40).
You slip out of the tent and head to the ranger station (turn to page 18).

At first the Indian boy doesn't budge. Then he breaks into a grin. "Call the cavalry? That's a good one!" he laughs. "Almost as good as my 'Where are you going, paleface?'"

He gets down from the horse and introduces himself. "I'm Wind-of-Summer Skyhawk, from Lapwai, Idaho. But just call me Windy."

You sit down and visit with him and find out that his whole family, plus three hundred other Nez Perce Indians, is camped out behind the museum. They're following the path of their ancestors, who came this way in 1887 with Chief Joseph on their way to Canada. "That's why I'm dressed this way. It's like one big, long parade," he concludes.

It's all so fascinating. You'd like to hear more. You wish now that you would have remembered to bring your camera.

"Say," Windy continues, "why don't you come on over to our camp and meet my granddad? He is president of the tribal council, so he could tell you a lot more about our people."

Just then a series of explosions ring out from down the street.

Choices: You go with Windy into the Indian camp (turn to page 106).
You decline the invitation and head toward the noise in town (turn to page 67).

Just down the road a bizarre sight greets you. You spot the presidential limousine—and it's stuck in a muddy little ditch. There, trying to push the car out, are several secret service agents and the president himself.

"It's really him, and he's pushing his own car!" you exclaim to yourself.

Choices: You run over and help the president push the car (turn to page 114).

You stop and get a good photo of the president pushing the limo (turn to page 44).

The huge beaver sits up on its back feet and begins to motion to you with one of its front paws. It seems to be beckoning you to come along the edge of the marsh and on up the creek.

Choices: You rub your eyes, declare that you must be seeing things, and head back around the marsh to the log crossing (turn to page 10).

You decide to take the beaver's advice and head upstream (turn to page 42).

"Hey, this kid can play the drums." Tina breaks into Mike's monologue.

"Just what we need, an amateur," Mike responds.

"Give the kid a chance, Mike!" Tina says. "Besides, we do need the practice."

Reluctantly Mike agrees. Quickly you run back to your tent for your own sticks. You take them everywhere you go so you can practice on the table, trees, or the twins.

They let you adjust the beautiful set of drums to your own liking. Someone cranks up a portable generator for power, and Tina hands you some headphones. "We crank the amplifiers in these. That way the neighbors can't hear a thing except the drums," she says with a smile.

You stumble through the first number, but soon you forget your nervousness and can follow the tunes pretty well. When the session finally concludes, the mood in the tent is much happier.

"Well, kid, you did a good job. Not a great job, but a good job. How about it? You willin' to play with us for tomorrow night's concert?" Mike asks.

You enthusiastically agree. Just then you hear someone outside the tent calling your name. You excuse yourself and run out of the tent.

You are startled by what you see.

Turn to page 50.

The boys decide maybe there is something worth digging up, and offer to help you. But you decline the offer, telling them you can do just fine by yourself. (You have no intention of sharing the box's contents with anyone.)

Surprisingly, the boys leave you alone and go on up the trail towards camp. You continue to dig. With the help of the snow marker, the box is soon freed and starts to float downstream. You lunge after it and slip in the creek. Now you are soaking wet, but you have the box.

You find your mystery tin impossible to open with your hands. It is sealed tightly. You head back to camp to get some of your dad's tools to open it up. But as you come around the bend you are taken aback by what you see.

Go to page 65.

Soon you are back to a well-marked trail, and the beaver has somehow disappeared in the brush. "Just as well," you say to yourself. "It's crazy to think he was motioning to me."

A shiny red reflection from the water's edge catches your attention. It's a six-pack of soft drinks. At first you believe that the cans are probably empty, some careless hiker's litter. But further investigation shows they are all full, and the six-pack is carefully lodged in the rocks with the cold water racing over them.

"Some fisherman's, I suppose," you say under your breath. You are suddenly a lot thirstier than you were a minute ago. "Boy, one of those would taste good."

You walk up the trail a bit, but see no one. "Maybe someone did forget them," you tell yourself. "No reason to let them go to waste."

You feel a bit guilty as you pull one can out of the plastic holder. Maybe you should wait for the fisherman to come back, and ask to buy one.

Choices: You take one of the sodas (turn to page 49).
You wait a few moments to see if someone comes back (turn to page 58).

The stagecoach is a real beauty, fully restored and hitched to six huge horses. You investigate the whole rig, and see no one around looking after it. You figure they must give rides around town, and wish you could find out where to get tickets.

Since it's parked next to a bank, you think maybe it's a promotion for the bank and that tickets are sold inside.

Choices: You go inside the bank to find out (turn to page 47).
You climb inside the coach and wait for someone to arrive, assuring yourself of the first ride (turn to page 62).

Just as you finish, one of the secret service agents sees you, runs over, and grabs your camera. "Hey, you're not supposed to do that!" he yells.

The president intervenes. "Come over here," he says to you. "Is that a Polaroid? Well, let me see your picture."

Sheepishly you hand him your photo.

"That's a great picture. Look at this, Byron," he says to one of the agents. "This would be a great publicity shot."

The president turns back to you. "I'll make you a trade. If you let me have this photo, I'll have Byron take one of you and me sitting here in the limo. What do you say?"

You quickly agree. Byron uses your camera, and the photo turns out beautifully.

It takes all the strength you can muster not to tell your family at supper later that night. But you wait

till campfire time, when everyone shares stories.

Carrie tells of an Indian she met. Dad tells about a bank holdup. Uncle Bill saw Buck Slade, the movie star, down by Old Faithful geyser. Cherrie said the ranger told her an old miner died up in the hills. And cousin Scott claims to have seen a brand-new geyser.

You casually pull out the picture and state, "Well, I just spent the afternoon visiting with a friend."

They are all amazed. The twins think the photo is a phony. The next morning they think differently. Your picture of the president pushing his car appears on the front page of the newspaper. Under the picture is the photo credit in clear letters: YOUR name!

THE END

Just as you open the bank door, several loud explosions ring out. It sounds like gunfire.

"Someone's shooting!" you hear a woman scream.

Choices: You go on into the bank to see what is going on (turn to page 57).
You quickly run out of the bank and hide in the bushes next to the stagecoach (turn to page 70).

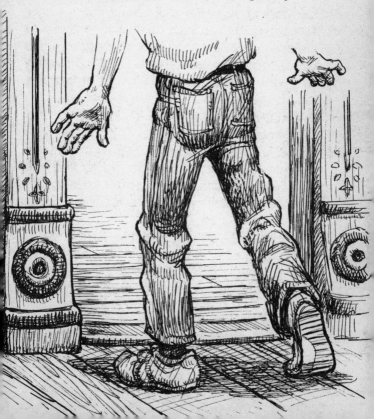

Thirty minutes later, you sit down on a rock to rest. "Nothing fits," you exclaim to yourself. "I must have measured from the wrong tree."

But by now it's too late to rectify your error. You are not sure where the cabin is. Even north and south are a bit fuzzy in your mind. You climb the nearest mountain to try to get your bearings.

As you enter a little lightning-cleared bald spot on top of the mountain, you spot a large bird sitting in a burned-out tree. Cautiously approaching, you hold your camera up and get a shot just as the bird flaps its wings to fly away. It's huge, some two feet long with a wingspan you'd guess at nearly six feet. It effortlessly glides towards a lake in the distance, and you marvel at its grace. Is it a hawk? An osprey? An eagle?

As you watch it soar in the air, the words of a Bible memory verse come into your mind, something about "mount up with wings as an eagle."

"That's what I really need to do to find this mine—fly!" you say to yourself. You decide to call off the search today and start it back at the cabin tomorrow.

Off to the left, you can see a lookout tower. If there's a ranger in it, he'll be able to guide you to camp. However, in the opposite direction you think you can see the creek and your trail.

Choices: You head over to the ranger's lookout (turn to page 80).
You strike out toward the creek and trail (turn to page 51).

As you finish drinking the soda, you hear a shout from up the creek. "Hey, kid! What do you think you're doing?"

You look up to see an older man hurrying down the trail toward you, with a fishing rod on one arm and a clenched fist on the end of the other. Your first impulse is to throw down the can and run up the hill into the trees. He's probably too old to make it up after you.

On the other hand, you think to yourself, you did take his drink. Maybe you should stay put and admit it. Perhaps paying him for it will make it easier.

He just turned the last bend. Now's the time to act.

Choices: **You confess, offer to pay him back, and return around the marsh to the log crossing (turn to page 10).**
You head for the woods as fast as your legs will carry you (turn to page 51).

It's your Uncle Bill and family.

"Where have you been?" Scott asks.

"Er, visiting the neighbors. They let me play their drums, and—" You are interrupted by your cousin Steve.

"Too bad. You missed seeing the president," he reports.

"Who?" you exclaim.

"The president of the United States, that's who. We just saw him and he waved right at me," Steve declares.

"Well, enough of that. Where's our camping site?" Aunt Judy asks.

"Oh, no," you mutter. "I'll be right back!"

You run up to the ranger station. A "Sorry, We're Full" sign greets you. You beat on the window and get the ranger's attention. He takes the fees for your family's campsite, but tells you there's no room left for your uncle's family.

"How about site 19? It's empty," you plead.

"Nope. It's reserved. Those folks will be in tonight, or in the morning at the latest."

Choices: You tell the ranger your predicament and ask his advice (turn to page 56). You go back and tell your uncle that they have site number 19, hoping to think of another solution before the real occupants get there (turn to page 130).

You decide to cut back through the woods to the next mountain, then down to the trail and back to camp. You've had enough for one day.

But the next mountain is further away than it looked, and fallen trees block your way at every turn. By the time you reach the hill, the sun is setting behind the high mountains to the west. You hurry to where the trail should be.

But there's no trail! "I'm lost," you murmur in disbelief.

You can't even find a creek, so you have no idea which direction to go.

"This is the dumbest thing I've ever done!" you say, and you can almost hear the twins making that same comment. You do have some dry matches, and build yourself a small fire next to an old hollowed log. You crawl into the log to spend the night. In the morning you plan to add green branches to make the fire smoke. Perhaps that will signal your location to others.

"Boy, what a way to start a vacation!" you sigh as you fall asleep.

THE END

You find out that "chuck" is really a first-class smorgasbord. You load up your plate and look for a place to sit. Finally you sit down next to a pretty lady in a fluffy violet western dress. She has just been seated herself.

"Say, are you a big movie star?" you ask. "I mean, are you one of the main ones?" Suddenly you realize what you said, and blush.

She smiles. "Don't be embarrassed. I know what you mean. And no, I guess I'm not a star. I'm what they call a feature spot. A supporting role."

"Well, that sounds great to me," you stammer. "Sorry I asked that way."

"Oh, don't worry. Say," she continues, "how about you and I asking a blessing before we eat?"

She bows her head and begins to pray. You bow your head, too. When she finishes, you both begin to dig in.

Choices: You ask her if she is a Christian (turn to page 84).
You hurry through your meal and wave good-bye to her as you run back to watch for Buck again (turn to page 60).

"Hey, relax! I was only joking," the young Indian replies. "You don't think we run around saying things like that, do you?"

You smile cautiously as he laughs and climbs off the horse. "My name's Windy. I'm a Nez Perce Indian from Idaho. A bunch of us are over here to retrace the route our people took when they followed Chief Joseph up towards Canada, so that's why we're in costume and everything. It's been like one big, long parade. But I'm ready to get home. It's about time for the baseball league to start."

You nod politely. "We're just here on vacation."

"Hey, want to ride my horse?" the boy offers. "His name is SlamDunk. I named him myself."

"Sure!" You stand up on a trash can and climb aboard the blanketed horse. Windy crawls up behind you. You both head over to the museum where you not only view the white buffalo, but also see a multimedia show all about Windy's people. It's quite fascinating, and you want to hear more.

"Why don't you come over to our camp?" Windy suggests. "My granddad is president of the tribal council. He could tell you a lot more."

You're ready to go with Windy when you glance at your watch and see that your hour is up. Your folks will soon be expecting you back at the car.

Choices: You go on with Windy for just a little while (turn to page 106).
You regretfully decline, and go on back to the car (turn to page 125).

No, it's not another Bigfoot. "Unbelievable," you mumble to yourself. You're looking up at a ten-foot grizzly bear! It's up on its hind legs growling at the monster man.

Another rock comes flying by you. This one hits its mark: the bear. The giant brown grizzly starts to run straight towards Bigfoot. The monster retreats right down the middle of the creek, turning to heave another stone at the oncoming bear. This time the rock hits with a resounding thud. The bear stops suddenly, turns, and flees into the woods. Meanwhile, Bigfoot continues around the bend in the creek.

You've been holding your breath all this time. Now you relax—and slam your right fist into your left hand. "Why didn't I get a picture!" You could almost scream.

Cautiously you proceed down the creek to follow the monster, but his hike in the water insured that he would leave no tracks. You can't find his trail anywhere.

The grizzly's tracks are easy to spot, since they lead up to the woods. "A picture of that bear could be better than no photo at all," you reason to yourself.

Choices: **You continue to look along the creek for a sign of the Bigfoot monster (turn to page 68).**
You decide to follow the bear tracks up into the woods (turn to page 111).

56

The ranger smiles. "Got yourself in a fix, eh? Well, I happen to know that the folks in 24 will be moving on tomorrow. So I'll let your uncle and family camp with you in 23 tonight, and then tomorrow they can have 24 after the others leave."

You hurry back and confess your mix-up to your uncle and aunt. They laugh and start to unload their gear. Your dad is not quite so happy, and you end up on dishwashing duty that night.

Around the campfire, everyone shares the day's adventures. Cherrie had a run-in with a real Indian in West Yellowstone. Your dad was at the bank when some guys dressed up like cowboys, robbed it, and fled in a stagecoach, of all things. Scott and Steve told about waving to the president. Then they all turn to you.

"And what exciting thing did you do today?" someone asks.

Choices: **You tell them about your audition with the rock group (turn to page 64).**
You keep your tv appearance a secret and say, "Oh, I just visited with the neighbors" (turn to page 90).

Before you can look around the bank, a man waving a gun runs toward you. He grabs your shoulder, spins you around, and yells, "If anyone follows us, I'll shoot this kid."

He drags you out the door and pushes you into the stagecoach. Two other gunmen appear from the bank, and one hops up and gets the rig headed down the street. Soon it is dodging cars and headed out of town.

Choices: You bite the man's hand who is holding you and take a chance at diving out the stagecoach window (turn to page 93).

You grab your throat and say in a loud voice, "Oh, my mumps are really hurting bad!" (turn to page 121).

As you sit by the water's edge, you hear someone coming toward you. Looking up, you see an older man with a reel strapped to his belt and fishing rod in hand.

"Hi. How are you doin'?" he greets.

"Fine, thanks. Did you get any fish?" you ask.

"Sure did. Look at these beauties."

"Boy, those are the biggest trout I've ever seen," you say sincerely. "And pretty, too."

"There's a bigger one in there. I just couldn't land him. Care for a cold drink?" When you nod, the man throws one of the coveted drinks to you. "I suppose you are on vacation," he continues.

"Yessir. How about you?"

"It's my day off. I'm a park ranger here. This is the best fishing hole in all Yellowstone. Did you ever fish with flies?" he asks.

You admit you haven't.

"Well, come on, I'll teach you—unless you think you should head on up the trail."

You think about it for a moment. A big trout would really impress your family, with the possible exception of Cherrie. You glance up the trail and suddenly see the big beaver motioning to you.

"Did you see that?" you blurt out to the ranger.

He turns his head, but the beaver is once again gone. Weird beaver or giant trout? It's your choice.

Choices: You learn how to fly-fish (turn to page 63).
You follow the beaver (turn to page 71).

You limp on down the trail, pretending to be injured, until the boys are far out of sight. Then you return to the creek and the tin box. In a few moments you have the box in your hands, but you slip on a mossy rock as you head back to shore. You land flat on your back in the stream, but manage to hold on to the box.

Once back to shore you pound on the box with a rock. The lid won't budge. There's nothing to do but head back to camp.

As you come around the first bend in the trail, you stop dead in your tracks.

"Oh, no!" you say, mumbling under your breath.

Turn to page 65.

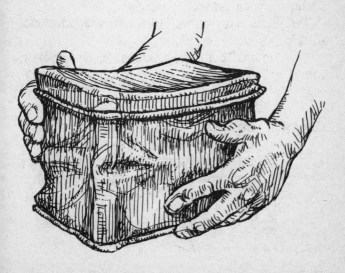

A sudden explosion at one end of the canyon catches your attention. They are starting the filming at a fake mine shaft! You see Buck coming out of the mine, and dust flying everywhere. Then, all of a sudden, it's over. It was only a two-minute shot.

Buck walks toward you and calls out, "Hey, kid, come here." You hurry over and find him talking to a woman named Jill.

"If they aren't here, we'll have to wait," she is saying.

"I say we don't wait! Why not use this kid?" Buck growls.

"I'm sure Jodi and Dean will be along any minute," Jill interjects.

"We can't hold up production for two extras who would rather look at a moose than show up on time," Buck growls.

"But, Buck, you know the Guild will have our scalps if—"

"Sign up the kid. I'll pay his dues. Now let's get on with it. You can ride a horse, can't you?" Buck asks you.

Choices: You nod your head yes, even though you've never ridden (turn to page 97).
You apologize and say you really don't know how (turn to page 86).

The map is extremely accurate. The three boulders are right where they should be, as well as the scrub brush and the fallen log. Clearing back some deer brush you find yourself staring at a mine entrance about four feet high.

You can't help noticing a large, crudely painted sign guarding the entrance. "Warning! Keep out! Or be shot!"

As you stand trying to figure out your next move, you hear a noise from inside the mine. It sounds like singing, or maybe screaming. You can't tell which.

Choices: **You heed the sign, take a picture of the mine entrance, and head back to camp (turn to page 79).**
You slowly creep into the mine, straining to listen for those sounds (turn to page 88).

You sit in the coach only a minute when you hear some explosive sounds coming from the bank. You see three men flee from the building, one holding a gun on a very frightened young girl. You dive out the door of the coach just as they approach from the other side.

As the vehicle starts to pull away, the frightened girl's eyes meet yours. "Help me!" she screams. Then a big hand covers her mouth, and she disappears inside the stage.

Choices: You make a lunge for the back of the stagecoach (turn to page 89).
You grab a dirt bike that's parked on the sidewalk and start to follow (turn to page 83).

Ranger Marshall turns out to be an excellent teacher. You're a city kid whose only experience with a rod and reel was with your grandpa at the lake. But you catch on fast.

Soon you're able to cast across the creek to a small pool where the ranger claims the big one is hiding. A half hour and another soft drink later, a yank on the line almost pulls you into the frigid water. You rapidly reel in the line, but Mr. Marshall yells at you to slow down. You listen to his careful instructions.

"One that big can snap the line and even break the pole. Take it real steady and gentle or you'll never have him in the frying pan," he instructs.

You pull as slowly as you can. The fish fights with surprising strength. But twenty minutes later you land a whopper. The ranger hooks his pocket scale to a nearby limb and weighs the fish.

"Would you believe that?" he exclaims, "A ten-pound trout! That old boy must have been in that hole for years. Not bad for your first try."

As the two of you take your catch back to camp the ranger promises to stop by and confirm the story to your family. "Otherwise, the twins will never believe I really caught this," you explain as you carry your prize in full view.

THE END

Everyone is excited at the news of your tv appearance.

The next morning you visit with Tina. They're going down to the lodge to set up for the concert. They want you to be there by 3:00 P.M.

"Are you nervous?" she asks.

"Sure I am," you reply. "But then I prayed about it all night long, so the Lord's helped me relax a little."

"Say, are you into that religion stuff?" she asks.

Choices: You decide to tell her about your Christian faith (turn to page 77).
You say, "Oh, it's no big deal. I always pray when I'm nervous. Doesn't everybody?" (turn to page 76).

Blocking the trail ahead of you are the three boys. The red-haired one grabs you by the shirt. You pull away and the shirt tears. This isn't going to be easy. The three are demanding you give them the box.

You want to slug the red-haired guy in the face. But what about the other two?

Choices: **You slug the red-haired kid (turn to** **page 72).**
You jump into a fake karate pose and yell, "I hope you guys have good insurance coverage. I didn't get this black belt for playing checkers" **(turn to page 81).**

"Hey, let's go see what that noise was," you call to Windy.

"OK," he concedes. "But it will be quicker if you hop up on old SlamDunk."

"Who?"

"My horse, SlamDunk," he laughs.

It seems really weird. Here you are, riding with an authentically dressed Indian on a pinto horse through tourist traffic, down the middle of a paved street.

But that isn't as strange as the sight coming toward you. It is a fully rigged stagecoach pulled by six big horses. The rig narrowly misses hitting an old pickup truck and rounds the corner behind you.

You thought you saw a frightened little girl in the back of the stagecoach. "You think we should follow the stage?" Windy asks.

Choices: You turn around and follow the stagecoach (turn to page 85).

You proceed in the direction you started, to where you heard the explosions (turn to page 78).

68

Your persistence pays off. After a half hour of searching the creek bank, you spot the big track once again. Just as you start to follow it, you hear a high-pitched scream from the other side of the water.

"Hey, over there, what's the problem?" you call out.

Suddenly a little girl about eight appears on the other side. "I got my hook stuck in Bobby's foot, and we can't get it out," she sobs. "I think he's really hurt."

"Where are your parents? Can't they help?" you call back.

"Please, we need somebody now," she cries. "I think he's dying!"

"Oh, brother," you think. "He can't die from a fish-hook in the foot. Besides, I can't leave Bigfoot's trail now, or I may never catch up with it."

"Please hurry!" the girl whines. She's practically hysterical now.

Choices: **You tell the girl to head on back to camp and find help, and you con-tinue after the Bigfoot (turn to page 73).**
You abandon your trail and cross the creek to help the little girl and Bobby (turn to page 94).

Before long you realize the dirt road is leading you nowhere. Not only that, you hear cheering from the other side of the hill. The president is passing by, and you've missed seeing him.

Disgusted, you turn to go back to camp when you notice a faint puff of smoke or steam coming up out of the ground next to an old log off to the left. As you get closer you feel the ground under-foot start to tremble and shake. The steam gets stronger and more violent looking.

Suddenly a one-foot hole cracks open in the ground and grows larger and larger. The earth looks like it's about to explode. The shaking knocks you to your knees. As the bright blue hole grows larger, it is now only a few feet away from you. "Oh, no! A volcano!" you shout, but no one can hear you. You remember studying about Mount St. Helens in school just this year.

Choices: You run down the road as fast as you can away from the eruption (turn to page 74).
You go up the hill a short ways and get your camera set to take some pictures (turn to page 92).

Safe for a moment behind the bush, you get a ringside view of the action. A tall man wearing an old brown cowboy hat bursts out of the bank door. His face, disguised by a nylon stocking, is as fearsome as the gun he waves in his hand.

Right behind him come two other gunmen. One is carrying a small blue duffel bag. The other is holding a young girl hostage. The frightened child tries to kick her way to freedom, but a strong rough hand tosses her into the stagecoach. As it starts to pull away, the girl tries one last chance at freedom. Her frightened face appears at the stagecoach window, and suddenly she spots you behind the bushes. Before the gunman's hand clamps around her mouth, she manages a weak "Help me! Help me, please!"

Choices: You make a lunge for the back of the stagecoach (turn to page 89).
You grab a dirt bike you see parked on the sidewalk, and start to follow (turn to page 83).

For close to an hour and a half you follow the big beaver. He's always up the trail a couple hundred feet in front of you. Whenever you think you're gaining on him, he hides in the brush and then in a few moments appears far in front of you.

Finally you see him turn off the trail, cut through some thick underbrush, and head into a little cavelike opening in the mountain. As you stand and peer inside you notice you can see daylight at the other side. "It's a tunnel!" you exclaim.

This tunnel is so small you would have to crawl through it on your hands and knees. You see water dripping down inside it and mud on the tunnel floor. Yuck. You've about decided to return down the trail when you hear a voice echo down the tunnel. "Come on! Come on!"

Startled, you look closer. It's the beaver talking. "I said, hurry up!"

Choices: You say "That's it. I'm suffering from heatstroke," and return to see if the ranger will still teach you how to fly-fish (turn to page 63).

You decide you'll try to crawl through the tunnel (turn to page 82).

It was a dumb move. Instantly a fist slams into your stomach, and then another catches you on the side of the face. Soon the boys have your tin box, and you're on the ground with nothing but aches and pains.

They pry the box open. "The laugh's on you, kid," they exclaim. "There's nothing in here but rags and old papers." They throw the box to the ground, papers and all, and head up the trail.

As soon as you get your breath back, you gather up the contents and head for camp yourself.

Turn to page 91.

The tracks of Bigfoot lead to a mountain of loose granite rock. You begin to pick your way up the hill, hand over hand. Then your left foot slips and you begin to slide backwards. Suddenly it seems as if half of the mountain is crashing down on top of you. You started a small avalanche!

The rocks flow around your feet, pinning you to your tracks. You can't move!

Just as you're figuring out what to do next, you look up and see the monster coming down the slope towards you. You try to scream, but nothing comes out of your mouth.

Turn to page 100.

You keep running right up the hill and start yelling at the remnants of the crowd.

"Volcano! Volcano!" you scream.

They ignore you. You run all the way back to the ranger station by your camp. "There's a volcano erupting over near the highway! It's not one of the geysers, because it was right next to the dirt service road."

The ranger smiles. "Don't worry, kid. There's no volcano around here. Now go relax."

"Really, I'm not kidding. You've got to believe me," you plead. Finally the ranger relents and calls headquarters.

"Say, you guys heard about any unusual thermal activity near the service road? Really? No kidding? That's great! Sure, I'll post a notice. How soon can folks go over? Right." The ranger hangs up the phone and turns to you.

"Well, kid, there's no volcano. But it is a new geyser. It's been quite a few years since we had a new one. They're going to name it after the president. Too bad you didn't get a picture of its formation. That would have been something."

You look down at the camera hanging around your neck, "You klutz!" you say to yourself. "Why didn't I stop and take a picture?"

"I guess that's the way adventures go," you mutter as you head back to camp. "Sometimes you miss them by just a hair."

THE END

"Well, I don't pray, but maybe I should," she replies.

You change the subject.

The day passes slowly as you await your big opportunity. Your folks take you down early. Then Tina comes over looking glum.

"They bumped us, kid," she states flatly.

"What?" You are shocked.

"They decided they had too many acts, and they bumped us, that's all. That's the way it goes."

"Can they do that?" you ask.

"They just did." She shrugs. "The guy did say we could set up our equipment and wait around to see if one of the other groups falls through. But that's a crummy way to treat us. We're leaving."

"Where are you going?" your father asks Tina.

"Back to Boise, I guess," she says.

Choices: You reluctantly say good-bye to Tina and the others (turn to page 128).
You try to convince them to wait it out, just in case there's a chance (turn to page 126).

"Well, I guess I'm into religion," you tell Tina. "I mean, it's not just religion. It's Jesus Christ."

"Hey, that's great!" Tina replies. "I like Jesus, and all those other prophets, too."

Choices: You nod your head and change the subject (turn to page 132).
You take time to tell Tina why Jesus is not just one of the prophets (turn to page 116).

You notice that up ahead there is a crowd around the bank entrance. The two of you climb down off of SlamDunk, and Windy asks what happened. "Bank's been robbed," someone hollers back.

"Hey, maybe that Indian's in on it," another yells.

"Yeah! I told the mayor they shouldn't let those Indians camp over there," another protests.

Windy whirls around. "That does it!" he tells you. "I'm leaving. You stay and investigate. These are your people, anyway, not mine." He runs to Slam-Dunk.

"Wait a minute!" You follow him. "I sure don't claim that type of people as my kind." You crawl up behind Windy on the old pinto, and he offers no protest.

Neither of you speak as you ride toward the museum and the Indian encampment.

"Hey, listen, Windy. I'm sorry about what those people said about Indians," you tell him.

"Don't worry about it. It's not the first time, or the last." He sighs. "Here's where we met, friend. I'll help you down."

Somehow you just don't feel right about leaving. So you hesitate, then say, "Er, Windy? Hey, I'd really like to go and talk with your grandfather, like you mentioned. Would you mind?"

"Aren't you afraid of getting scalped, pale-face?" Windy laughs as the two of you head toward his family's encampment.

Turn to page 106.

You hike only a few yards down the trail when your curiosity—and your conscience—overcome you. You return to investigate the mine.

Turn to page 88.

It takes longer than you imagined to reach the lookout. As you approach, the ranger calls out from the platform for you to come on up. One hundred and twelve grueling steps later you are in the tower, viewing the majesty of the mountains through the ranger's telescope.

"Say," the ranger says. "I've got some repairs to make on the supply shack down there. How about you staying up here for a little while, looking out for fires, while I go down to the ground and do some work?"

You agree readily. But the job is not as exciting as you thought. Sitting there staring at treetops isn't all that great. Then you sight something. Is it dust, or could it be smoke? As it curls upward you realize a fire really is breaking out. Quickly you call the ranger. He scampers up the steps, charts the fire, and calls it in on the radio.

"Great work, kid!" We'll catch that one in time," he says.

When the fire crews complete their work, they stop by the ranger station. He asks them to give you a ride back to camp, which you are happy to have.

When you arrive back at camp, Carrie asks about your ride in a Park Service fire rig. "Where have you been?"

"Oh, just spotting forest fires," you reply casually.

THE END

"No scrawny kid's going to bluff me," the red-headed guy responds.

"Wait a minute, Tony. Maybe he does know karate," another of the boys says cautiously. "Besides, who wants an old tin can, anyway? Probably just has a rotten sandwich inside."

They decide to go on up the trail and leave you alone, none too soon. "I couldn't have faked that karate stuff much longer," you laugh to yourself.

As you walk back to camp, you finally manage to open the box and discover some oily rags wrapped around some old papers. It's hardly the secret treasures you hoped for, but maybe a park ranger can tell you about them.

Turn to page 91.

The tunnel is a slimy mess to crawl through, but you soon forget the trouble when you get out on the other side.

Before you stands a lush, green valley, with sheer mountain cliffs on every side. In the middle of the valley is a clear blue lake, making a perfect reflection of the distant snowcapped mountains.

Cascading over one of the cliffs is a small waterfall. But the sun's rays are at such an angle that it looks like a waterfall of rainbows. You reach for your camera.

"Come over here; you can get a better picture," the beaver's voice says.

Turn to page 96.

The dirt bike is a Yamaha, just like yours at home, so you have no trouble starting it. Just then a voice to your right catches your attention.

"Hold it right there, kid, or I'll shoot!"

You turn and are terrified to see a sheriff holding a gun right at you. A frantic bank teller stands next to him. "That must be one of them, sheriff, trying to get away by stealing Christie's motorcycle!"

"Sir, the robbers are getting away in that stage, and they have a hostage, so I was merely trying to—" you manage to stammer.

"Cut the talk, put your hands against the wall, and spread your feet," the gun-toting officer demands.

You comply. For the next hour and a half you talk to the authorities. But it is not until your dad shows up that they finally believe your story. All the way back to camp you receive a stern lecture from your parents about the foolishness of trying to do a policeman's job, and about how "borrowing" someone's dirt bike is never right.

"Well, maybe so," you say, "but at least I had a real adventure today. That's more than what would have happened if I'd stayed in camp."

That's what you think until you hear the twins' story: some incredible account about being in a movie with Buck Slade!

"Bummer!" you say. "Maybe going to town wasn't such a great idea after all."

THE END

"Say, are you a Christian?" you ask.

"Yes, I am. Does that surprise you?" she returns.

"Well, it's just . . . I mean, I didn't think people in the movie business . . ." you stammer.

"You didn't think show business folks were ever interested in spiritual matters?" she laughs.

"I'm sorry," you mutter sheepishly.

"Don't be. Everyone thinks the same thing. All they read about is wild parties, immoral relationships, and constant bickering. And that's true to some extent, but it's not the whole story. Movie people are just a mixture of regular folks like any other industry. There are saints and sinners alike. Say, are you a believer, too?" the pretty actress asks.

"Yes," you reply. "I've believed in Jesus ever since I was little."

"Well, that's smarter than me," she comments. "I went to church for years before I really got to know Jesus as my Savior. Say, I know about something that may interest you."

She begins to scribble a note on her napkin. "7:30 P.M., Spruce Lodge. Back room."

"If you can," she says, "come on down to the Spruce Lodge tonight. You'll be really surprised. And, by the way, my name's Lea Ann."

Turn to page 95.

The tourist traffic prevents you from catching up to the stagecoach. But Windy spots its dusty tracks headed down an old forest service trail. And just a few yards down the trail is the stage itself.

Inside you find the frightened girl, who is babbling incoherently about robbers. You release her and try to calm her down while Windy spots some car tracks leading on down the trail.

"I think we should follow them," you tell Windy.

He hesitates, then says, "I don't know. Criminals are dangerous, and the girl is OK. Maybe we should just take her back and tell the police."

Choices: You return to town with the girl (turn to page 101).
You send Windy back with the girl, and you proceed down the trail on foot (turn to page 105).

"That's all right, kid," Buck grins. He leads you over to the director. The man, whom Buck calls Brett, carefully describes what you must do. You will run out of the fake barn and up toward the little house just as Buck rides in from the east. All you have to do is yell, "Buck! Buck!"

Brett, the director, then sends you over to wardrobe and to the makeup trailer. It takes about an hour, but finally you are ready to appear on the set. You feel nervous.

It's only a short scene. Brett says it will only be a minute or two of actual film. But it takes a lot longer than that to film it.

The rehearsal takes at least an hour. Every camera must be carefully set, and every step exactly placed.

Finally all is ready. "This is the real thing, kid," Brett hollers.

"Action!" someone yells.

But there's no action.

Turn to page 112.

Even though it's quite dark inside, you are glad you decided to enter because now you can hear unmistakable cries for help. They're coming from somewhere off to your right.

You proceed slowly as your eyes adjust to the dim lighting. Finally you near your goal and see a flicker of light from an oil lantern. There's an old man there who looks pinned down by some large beams.

Suddenly he cries out, "Look out, kid! Get back!"

Turn to page 103.

You hold on to the baggage straps at the rear of the stagecoach and try to find footing for your shoes. As you round the first corner, one of the straps you're holding onto breaks off. You see that the other one's about to go, too.

The stage turns sharply to the right down an unused forest service trail, and as it does the second baggage strap rips from the seams. You go flying towards the tall weeds at the corner. After tumbling several times, you rise to your knees in time to see the robbers jump into a small brown Datsun pickup and head on up the trail. The abandoned stagecoach effectively blocks any other vehicle's pursuit.

You notice that the young girl is not with them. You rush over to the stage and find her inside, tied with leather belts and gagged with a nylon stocking. She is almost in tears as you free her.

"I knew you'd come save me. I just knew it from your eyes," she says, sighing in relief.

As the two of you walk out to the highway, she starts to say, "Hey, we didn't even introduce ourselves. My name is Julie. What's —"

"Hey, you two, hold it right there!" You both look startled to see a Gallatin County sheriff's car. "You kids get over here right now!" the officer yells.

Turn to page 127.

Later that evening, Mike comes over and calls out, "Hey, where's our new drummer?"

Carrie runs over to him before you can get him quiet. The secret's out. Everyone rejoices at your opportunity to be on tv.

When Mike leaves, Carrie and Cherrie are mad at you. "You were keeping this quiet just so we wouldn't get to meet those guys," Carrie complains. "Did you see that cute Mike stare at me?"

"Stare at you?" Cherrie scoffs. "I was the one he was interested in."

"You've got to be kidding!"

The fight continues to accelerate, but you slip away to your tent. "I've got more important things to do than worry about who's the 'fairest in the land,'" you laugh to yourself.

Turn to page 64.

The park ranger realizes the importance of your find. "These papers are signed by John Colter! Do you know what this means?"

You shake your head. John Colter? After the ranger calls the park headquarters, he turns to explain. "Professor Paul Way is coming down to take a look. Listen, kid, John Colter is reported to have been the first white man to set foot in the park. He was with Lewis and Clark on their exploration in 1805 and 1806, and then afterwards he took off on a trapping expedition of his own. There are reports from other sources that he discovered thermal springs and geysers, but he himself never wrote anything down. At least we didn't think so."

The ranger looks at your tin box. "If these are his papers, it would push firsthand knowledge of this area back almost fifty years!"

"Kid, I'll give you five hundred bucks cash for those papers." You turn to see a man in Bermuda shorts standing behind you.

"Don't be silly," the ranger responds. "Wait until Professor Way arrives."

"Why wait?" the other man says. "Maybe he'll prove them fakes, and you'll be out five hundred bucks. You'd better take my offer now; I won't make it again."

Choices: You sell the papers for five hundred dollars (turn to page 129).
You decide to wait for Professor Way (turn to page 108).

Your position on the hillside proves to be just perfect for photos. Fortunately for you, it turns out not to be a volcano, but rather a new geyser in the making. Your new Polaroid camera is able to get eight good shots of its formation.

About the time you finish, several park rangers arrive and begin to rope off the area.

"Kid, did you get some pictures?" one asks. You show them what you took.

"These are terrific!" a tall, blond-haired man responds. "I'm Dr. Arledge of the geological staff here at the park. These pictures are really invaluable. Do you mind if I take them and make some copies for scientific study? I'll bring them back to your camp tomorrow."

You quickly agree and head back to camp. Nobody believes your account, and the twins are mad that you didn't get a picture of the president. But they don't stay mad long.

The next morning at 10:30, Dr. Arledge shows up with a reporter from a local newspaper. Your family stands in awe as the scientist returns your pictures.

"Look here!" He hands you the morning edition of the paper, and there, covering half the front page, is one of your pictures of the geyser.

"Now, if you will stand over by your family," says the reporter, "I'd like to have a picture of the young person whose name will be attached to the newest geyser in the park."

THE END

"Yeoow!" the gunman yelps.

He throws you down to the floorboard of the stage and holds on to his aching hand. At this point it is futile to try to get to the window. But you've got to get away!

Choices: You kick at the man, and try once more to get the stage door open (turn to page 136).

You decide not to resist anymore, and wait for a better opportunity (turn to page 98).

Reluctantly you wade across the ice-cold creek toward the little girl. She is still in tears and sits huddled beside a little black dog.

"Where's your brother? Where's Bobby?" you ask her.

"My brother? Bobby's not my brother," she replies. "He's my puppy. Anyway, he pulled the hook out himself. See?"

"You mean I came all the way . . . " Tears come back to her eyes as you start to yell.

"Well, I caught this fish with the hook, and it died. And I thought Bobby might die when I caught him with a hook. I didn't want him to die."

You calm down a bit and sit on a rock. No reason to worry about that Bigfoot now. He's long gone.

The little girl continues. "What happens to dogs when they die? Do they go to heaven?"

Turn to page 113.

By the time you get back to the set, the filming is over. Buck walks over to you. "Did you get a good view of the action down at the mine? I do my own stunts, you know."

"Well," you confess, "actually, I missed it, Buck. You see, I was down at the cafeteria. I mean at 'chuck.' And I got to talking to Lea Ann, and—"

"No sweat, kid," he interrupts. "It was a short scene. Too short. A couple of bit players didn't show up, so we had to postpone shooting more until morning. Boy, is that director mad! It's a good time to leave. Say, I thought you might like these." Buck hands you several large autographed pictures of himself as you head towards his pickup.

"Thanks!" you exclaim, for a moment you get lost in looking at the pictures.

Soon you two pull up to your campsite. "Here you go, kid. I've got to run to town."

You start to leave, and then you remember your conversation with the actress. "Say, Buck, about this Lea Ann . . ."

"Lea Ann? She's a good woman. Yes, sir, a good woman. A little tricky perhaps, but—Oops! It's late. Got to run, kid; see you later." Buck heads down the drive.

"Good, but tricky?" you say to yourself.

Turn to page 122.

After taking several fantastic pictures, you sit down on a rock next to the beaver to rest. The beaver has started to say something to you when another big beaver waddles by.

"Hello, Mildred," your friend says. "Nice day."

"Why, Henry, how have you been? How's Kitty?" she asks.

"Mean as ever, mean as ever. Heh, heh!" he smiles. You think his smile looks rather peculiar. If he were human, you'd recommend braces for those front teeth.

"And who's the kid, Henry?" The she beaver points a paw at you.

"Oh, a good friend of mine from down the trail," Henry replies.

"Well, nice to meet you, Human. I must run now." She heads on down a small trail.

You sit there for a moment. Then for the first time you speak to the beaver. "I really don't believe this, you know."

"Believe what?" he asks.

"That I'm sitting here listening to some beavers talk. I mean, beavers don't talk!" you reply.

"Hmm," he says. "Now, that's an interesting theory. Interesting theory, indeed."

Turn to page 104.

The problem is that the only horse you've ever ridden was attached to a merry-go-round. But you figure you just can't pass up a chance to be in a movie.

Buck takes you over to the director, a man named Brett or Bart or something like that. He tells you what you are to do.

"Just ride up to the barn real slowly and dismount. Then when you see Buck ride up to the little house from the east, run over there yelling 'Buck! Buck!'" he instructs.

After an hour in wardrobe and makeup, you are ready for the shooting. The horse they bring you looks gigantic. One of the stunt men gives you a boost up.

"This is pretty simple, fellas," Brett yells. "Let's roll the cameras and see what we can get."

"Action!" comes the cry.

Not knowing exactly what to do, you copy what you've seen in the movies before. Kicking your heels into the horse's side, you jerk the reins and yell, "Giddap!"

Instantly you realize that's the wrong thing to do. The horse, instead of lazily walking up to the barn, takes off in a wild gallop past the little house and towards the hills. In the midst of your panic you see Buck riding alongside.

"Buck! Buck! Your shrill scream surprises even you.

Turn to page 99.

Soon the stagecoach stops and the gunmen tie you up with their belts and the nylon stockings they had used for masks. They do a good job. You can't move at all.

It seems like hours you lie there, but it is not more than twenty minutes before you hear someone holler, "Hey, here's the kid!"

It's an off-duty ranger named Oliver, who releases you and walks you over to his car. "The deputy had to pursue the bank robbers," he explains, "but he wanted me to take you back to town."

Your mom and dad are there at the bank when you return, and of course your mom starts to cry.

"Thank the Lord, you're OK," your dad sighs.

"I was thinking the same thing," you tell him in absolute sincerity. "Thank you, Lord!"

Turn to page 119.

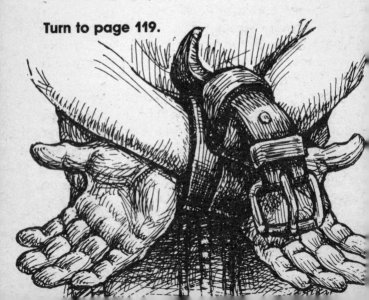

The whole nightmare passes with lightning quickness. Buck grabs the reins of your runaway horse and pulls them tight, then pulls you out of the saddle with his other arm.

Finally you can relax and get your breath. "Wow," you manage to say. "That was just like in the movies!"

"It is the movies," Buck says sternly. "But what was all that hogwash you gave me about knowing how to ride a horse?"

"Don't get mad at the kid," Brett interrupts as he walks over. "You all right?"

"Yeah. Look, I'm sorry I lied," you begin.

Brett interrupts once again. "Forget it, kid. You were great! We're changing the script, Buck. That was a great scene! We got the whole thing on the zoom from both sides. Terrific stuff. Wouldn't change it for the world."

Back in camp that night, you try to tell everyone about the day's events. They have a hard time believing your story. You don't blame them; you hardly believe it yourself.

The next day, around noon, Buck comes over to your camp and visits with your family. Suddenly everyone believes what you told them, because Buck has a large poster rolled up under his arm.

"Look at this, kid," he says. "The printshop did this last night. Ain't that something? It's a little rough, but they plan on using it for promotion purposes."

You just about faint when you see the photo.

Turn to page 133.

The monster reminds you of a shaggy, gray gorilla. "What's he going to do to me?" you wonder aloud.

Just then he puts a big, furry hand on your shoulder.

It's the last thing you remember.

Turn to page 109.

The two of you lead SlamDunk back to town, letting the girl, whose name is Julie, ride him. Turning the corner towards the bank, Windy brings the horse to a halt.

"This is the end of the line for me and SlamDunk," he says. "I'm not in the mood to visit with that crowd again."

Even though you and Julie protest, he won't change his mind. You head up the street and wander through the crowd. All of a sudden there's a shrill "Julie! My Julie!" as her mom comes running up to grab her.

"Hey, the girl's back and she's OK," someone yells.

"Kid, you're a hero!" A man pats you on the back as he talks. "Folks, we have a real hero here."

Everyone starts to applaud.

"Wait, wait," you protest. "Listen: it wasn't me. It was Windy's idea. He's the real hero."

"Windy?" someone questions.

"Yeah, the Indian boy on the horse."

"He kidnapped the girl?" another shouts.

The crowd was in an uproar. "Find that Indian!"

You climb up in the back of a truck and yell at the crowd. "I said Windy was the HERO! He saved Julie. Just ask her."

The people stand quiet for a moment, then start to disperse. As you head through the crowd, a man who had been hollering about the Indians grabs your arm.

Turn to page 131.

You look to where the old man is pointing and see a sagging timber above you. It's about ready to collapse. "If that one goes, the whole mountain will be on our heads," he hollers.

"But I've got to help you," you protest.

"Too late, too late—it's going now! Get out while you have a prayer of a chance!" he urges.

"We've both got a prayer of a chance," you return calmly. "It's all up to the Lord and this mountain." You cautiously crawl over to where he is and begin to pull off the beams.

"Broke my arm and I think my leg when these collapsed yesterday. Couldn't budge them," he mutters. "Thought no one could find me here. If you have the muscle, stick one of these beauties under that ceiling beam. Maybe that will give us some time."

You struggle to fit a giant brace under the sagging beam, but it doesn't quite fit. "What now?"

"Just grab that shovel by the lantern and try to dig down a little till the beam fits," he replies.

The ground proves almost impossible to dig. "It's too hard," you complain.

"Use the pick," comes the reply.

Chipping out a chunk of rock, you finally get the beam in place and help the miner get free from the partial cave-in that trapped him. "Boy, that was hard rock," you tell him.

"Let me see that rock," the old man says. "Well, I'll be dad-burned," he shouts. "Look at this!"

Turn to page 138.

"But then you can't help it, I suppose," this beaver named Henry continues. "Just a flaw in human nature."

"Er, uh, Mr. Beaver," you hear yourself stammer. "Do all beavers talk?"

"Of course! But not to people, mind you. We've got a vow of silence. Took it years ago. We promised the Lord to keep still and let you humans figure things out on your own. It's the plan he wanted. And by the way, you can call me Henry."

"You know God?" You're startled.

"Naturally. My word, it's only humans that are separated from him. It wasn't a beaver that ate the forbidden fruit in the Garden of Eden, you know."

He looks at the sun. "Well, I hate to end our chat, but if you don't start back soon, folks will come looking for you. Wouldn't want a bunch of people tramping around here. Come along, I'll show you the tunnel entrance."

"Say, er, Henry? If you have a vow of silence, how come you're talking to me now?" you ask.

Turn to page 137.

You walk on down the dirt roadway, not expecting to find much. After all, it would be impossible for you to catch up to a car, and if you did you wouldn't know what to do. The road gets very narrow and rough in places and you realize that the robbers must have a small car to make it through.

About then you decide to give up the hike and walk back to the road. "Just one more hill," you say. But as you crest the hill you see a small, brown pickup down below, stuck in a creek bed. You sneak down the hill to see what is happening.

You can only see two of the bank thieves. "We ain't got no choice. I say we gotta hike back to town and steal another car," says one.

"But that's like going into a lions' den," the other responds. "They'll be looking for us. What we need now is some cover."

"What about a hostage?" a deep voice booms right behind you. You turn quickly. The third robber is holding a gun on you!

Turn to page 135.

The Indian encampment holds many surprises for you. First, you notice it's not all that much different than your own camp. The grounds are filled with modern camping tents, pickup campers, travel homes, and horse trailers.

And second, you realize the conversation is no different than back home. All the boys talk about sports, and all the girls talk about boys.

Most of all you enjoy visiting with Windy's granddad. He seems pleased to have someone to listen to the history of the Nez Perce nation. You're lost in another of his tales when you realize you need to get back to the car to meet your folks.

"Why don't you ask them if you can spend the

night?" Grandpa Sam asks you. "We'll bring you back tomorrow. We have to go into the park for the big Fourth of July festivities."

You insist that Windy and his grandfather come with you when you ask. "I don't think they will let me go otherwise," you tell them.

Windy's granddad soon strikes up a conversation with your dad, and they seem to get along quite well. Then Grandpa Sam changes the topic of conversation, and you are completely taken aback by what he says.

Turn to page 118.

When the man in the Bermudas sees that you aren't about to sell him the papers, he stomps out to his travel home and heads north, muttering about a "dumb kid."

The ranger shakes his head. "I don't understand folks like that," he says. "History can't be bought. It belongs to all of us."

Professor Paul Way arrives and tentatively confirms your find. The papers are dated 1811-12, and the professor thinks they are genuine. They contain detailed descriptions of the park area. You donate the papers to the park museum. You also explain to the ranger about the broken snow marker, and make arrangements to pay for it.

Back at the campground, your whole family is impressed with your find. And several times during the next week, folks stop by to ask you how you found the papers.

The day before you leave to go home, Professor Way stops by and insists that the whole family come down to the museum. He proudly leads you over to a newly constructed glass case. There, properly displayed inside, are the Colter papers.

What you like best about the display is the brass plate attached to the outside. It reads, "The John Colter Papers, earliest written account of the Yellowstone region, discovered and donated to the museum by ..." And there it is. YOUR NAME!

"Two million folks a year will see that," you muse. "That's not bad. Not bad at all!"

THE END

A splash of cold water brings you around. Your sister Cherrie is standing above you. You notice that you are propped up against a tree, next to the creek, way back near the campgrounds.

"How'd I get here?" you ask.

"Don't try to talk your way out of this one," Cherrie warns. "Dad got worried about you and sent me to see if I could find you. I told him you were probably out playing hooky so you wouldn't have to help set up for dinner. And here's where I found you, right next to the creek, asleep. I'd think you could find a better place to hide."

"But, Cherrie, I wasn't hiding! I was up in the woods following this monster. You know, a Bigfoot? It was about to attack me, I think, and then all of a sudden—"

"Save it for dad," Cherrie snaps. "I'm not interested in your dreams. Come on, let's get back to camp."

The whole afternoon seems like a dream to you, too, until you look down at your camera. The rock-smashed Polaroid around your neck tells a different story. It didn't get that way from a nap by the creek.

But you suddenly realize that your camera might be the only one to believe your tale.

THE END

"Boy, this bear is dumb," you say to yourself after following the tracks awhile. "He must be lost. He's going around in circles."

Then it dawns on you. You spin around to see the bear lumbering up the trail behind you. He's been following you!

With lightning speed you scale the first tree you can reach and keep struggling up until you're high above the bear's reach. You're trying to remember: Can grizzlies climb trees?

Either they can't, or your prayers were answered. The bear stays on the ground. The trouble is, he stays there all afternoon and until dark. Just as you're wondering if you'll ever get down, you see some lanterns coming your way and hear people shouting your name. One voice sounds like Carrie's.

"Watch out, Carrie! Stay away! There's a bear right below this tree," you shout. The people all approach anyway. Their lights reveal that the bear is nowhere in sight.

"Oh, come on down, brave woodsman." she laughs, "What kind of story will you make up this time to cover up getting lost?"

You could tell them all about the bear, and Bigfoot, but what's the use?

"Hey, what are we having for dinner?" is your only comment.

THE END

"Cut!" Brett yells. "What's the matter, kid?"

"I guess I just am . . . scared," you reply.

"Well, let's try it again," he continues.

"Take two!" comes the cry.

This time you get started OK, but just as you round the front of the house you trip on the porch.

"Cut! Try it again," comes a voice.

Finally, six tries later, there's a "Cut! Print!" call, and the filming is over.

Later, heading back to camp with Buck, you apologize for all of your mistakes.

"No hassle, kid. It happens all the time. Why, last Friday we shot a fight scene twenty-one times before they liked it. Talk about tiring!" Buck laughs.

"Making movies is hard," you comment.

"Yeah, it's almost like working for a living." Buck laughs again as you leave his pickup and walk over to your family's camp.

"Where have you been?" Carrie questions.

"You wouldn't believe it if I told you," you reply.

"Oh, yeah? Try me," she insists.

"Well, I'll just say this: you can look for me in the next Buck Slade movie," you tell her.

"I don't believe you," she states flatly.

You just smile at her and go to see what's for dinner.

THE END

It seems funny, but all of a sudden you hear yourself teaching the little girl about death. "Well, I don't know about animals. But I know the Bible says that people who believe in Jesus go to heaven when they die," you tell her.

"What's heaven like?" she asks.

"We don't know," you answer. "But heaven is Jesus' home, so you know it must be nice. Also, he said he would get it ready for all people who believe, and then he promised to personally come and get us and take us there. Now that doesn't sound too bad, does it?"

"It sounds nice," she replies. "Will you help me find my way back to camp?" Apparently her attention span is pretty short.

The two of you walk silently up the trail. As you near the camp, she turns and says, "I love Jesus. So I'll get to heaven, won't I?"

"Well," you tell her with a smile, "you're on the right trail. You're certainly on the right trail."

THE END

You're not all that strong, but you must have provided the extra push needed, because soon the presidential car is out of the mud and back on the road.

"Hey, kid." A secret service agent collars you. "You aren't supposed to be down here, so you'd better get back up there with the crowd now."

"Now wait a minute, Byron," the president says. "We needed the help, and the kid gave it. What more could we ask? I think a little thanks is in order. Our country needs young people like this."

Then the president turns right to you. "Say, how about you riding with me in the limo down the parade route? I'd be pleased."

"But, Mr. President," the secret service man continues, "We don't have a security check on the kid."

"Security check! Good grief. Don't you trust anyone? I say the kid's going with me, and that's that. Provided you want to go."

You quickly nod yes, and before you know it you are traveling down the main road of Yellowstone National Park with the president of the United States. Thousands of tourists are waving and newsmen are taking pictures of the two of you.

Rounding a bend you see your cousins Scott and Steve in the crowd. They scream and wave at you, then point you out to Uncle Bill and Aunt Judy.

"Oh, no," you say to yourself. "It looks like Aunt Judy fainted. I guess people take awhile to get used to famous relatives."

THE END

You spend the next forty-five minutes telling Tina about who Jesus really was and what he did. She seems really interested.

That day and night before the tv appearance pass quickly. You feel in a daze as the lights flash, the cameras spin, the crowd roars, and the music blasts away. When the Idaho Blue Mountain Stampede goes on stage for a couple numbers, you improvise with the drums, and it seems to go over quite well. Spectacular fireworks end the show.

Afterward the group is excited. A record company executive in the audience contacted them to cut a record, and there is talk about a big promotional tour.

Mike and Tina spend half the night talking to you and your folks, trying to convince them to let you be a part of the band. Your parents are reluctant. You're too young, they say. Mike invites the

whole family to come along on the concert schedule. Your mother says you need to go to school.

Tina comes up with a compromise: you only have to stay with them for the rest of the summer. Then if you need to get out, it's OK. Your parents are weakening.

Finally Tina says, "Look, we really need the kid to be with us. This little drummer's the only one of us who's got things right with the Lord, you know what I mean? And we really need to know more about God. Now, how about it?"

Your parents finally agree to Tina's modified schedule. What a summer you now have planned! Playing the drums in a music group plus getting a chance to talk about God may be the best of all worlds.

THE END

After Grandpa Sam says it, you turn to Windy. "Your granddad is a preacher?"

"Yeah. But that's no big deal. So's my Uncle Walt," he replies.

"Are you a Christian?" you ask Windy.

"Sure. Most of my relatives are believers. Does that surprise you?" Windy asks.

"Well, yes, I guess. It's just—" you hear yourself mumble.

"Man, where have you been spending the last century?" Windy exclaims. "There have been believers in my family ever since the 1840s, my grandpa says. What about yours?"

"Well, I don't know. Probably not that long," you admit.

When the adults finish the conversation, the weekend is set. You get to spend the night with Windy and family. Then he is to come over to your camp tomorrow night, and on Sunday your whole family is driving into West Yellowstone to attend worship at the Nez Perce encampment.

Walking back to Windy's camp, you realize that summer vacation is going to hold even more excitement than you had hoped for.

"And to think," you say to yourself, "that I almost stayed in camp and let the twins come to town. Boy, would that have been a boring day!"

THE END

"Today was more adventure than I bargained for. You know, good old solitary boredom isn't so bad sometimes," you say to your mom as you carry the groceries over to the table back at the campsite. "Man, I'm glad to be back!"

Then, with uncharacteristic openness, you go over and hug Carrie and Cherrie. "I'm even glad to be back here with you two!" you hear yourself admit.

THE END

It takes awhile for you to get close enough to the funny little animal for another picture. He leads you over the next hill and down the valley.

Intently you stalk your prey. Like a good photographer, you forget everything except getting this picture. Finally the little fellow stops trotting, and you sneak up with camera ready.

"Hey, look at the cute little moose!" The voice startles you.

"Carrie! What are you doing out here?" you ask.

"What do you mean 'out here'? There's our campsite, great hunter," she says, pointing. "Mom, dad, Cherrie! Come look at this little moose I found," Carrie calls.

"What do you mean, YOU found?" you hear yourself saying.

"Well, I came down here looking for firewood, and that's when I spotted it. Look, it's eating the peanuts right out of my hand!"

Your anger bursts forth. "Carrie, I found that little moose, or whatever it is, and —"

"Oh, relax," she says. "I'll let you take a picture of me and my moose."

"That does it!" you tell her, and you sulk off towards your tent. You pass your mom, dad, and Cherrie going the other way.

"What kind of animal is down there?" your mom asks as you go by.

"A dork!" you reply irritably. "A real dork . . . and a baby moose, too."

THE END

"The mumps?" The man with the gun immediately pushes you to one side of the stagecoach. You hold your breath to puff out your cheeks and try to make it look real.

It works. The man quickly kicks open the stage door and gives you a shove. Before you know it, you are rolling head over heels in the tall weeds along the side of the road. When you come to, about half an hour later, you feel like you just played the Dallas Cowboys—without pads!

You head back to town.

"Where have you been?" your mother demands as you approach the car. "Your father and I have waited almost an hour, and you've been rolling in the dirt! Why, I ought to—"

You don't reply. You don't have to. You collapse into unconsciousness.

Ten days later you check out of the Bozeman hospital. Your bruises and head concussion are sufficiently improved to allow you to go home.

"Boy, what a story I'll have for the old 'What did you do last summer?' essay," you realize. "And besides, that neat candy striper named Connie said she'd write to me every week."

THE END

That night you convince your folks to let you go down to Spruce Lodge. The twins doubt your whole story about Buck and Lea Ann, but insist on going with you, supposedly in order to expose your wild account.

When you knock on the door, a large man with long, black hair opens it and stares at you.

"Uh, Lea Ann invited me—er, us," you reply.

A big grin covers his face. "Oh, sure, come in. We're glad to have you here."

As you enter, you notice about a dozen folks seated around a fireplace, most holding books in their hands. Lea Ann gets up to greet you. You introduce her to your sisters, but they just stand staring at a man sitting in an old rocking chair.

"I thought this might surprise you," Lea Ann comments. "You know, coming to a Bible study of movie industry people."

"A Bible study?" You are surprised. Then you notice who the twins are staring at. It's Buck! You walk over to sit down next to him.

"Don't worry about feeling uncomfortable, kid," he chides. "This is my first time here, too. Like I said, Lea Ann is a tricky woman." He winks. "But I don't mind."

THE END

The box won't budge, even after several minutes of struggle.

You decide to give up on it and follow those big tracks down the trail.

Turn to page 11.

When you get back to the car you find that your mom and dad have not finished shopping. So you wander through the shops to look for a present for the twins' birthday. You can't find anything you can afford, but you do find an ice-cream shop. At the table near the doorway you notice several kids your own age.

You'd like to visit with them, but first you go over to buy an ice-cream cone. Trying to act as cool as possible to impress the others, you order two scoops of Peaches and Pralines. As you're walking casually towards the group, a little kid darts in front of you, hitting your elbow. Suddenly there's a large lump of Peaches and Pralines sliding down the front of your shirt. All the kids at the table laugh.

You quickly leave the ice-cream shop and hurry to the car. "What a mess," you mutter as you scoot down in the car seat, hoping no one else will see your new attire.

When your folks show up, they aren't much help. "You really ought to use a cone or a cup and spoon when you eat ice cream," your dad comments with a laugh. You change the subject and mention the Indian boy you met.

"Well, maybe you'll see him Sunday," your mom replies. "We saw a poster in the supermarket mentioning a worship service at the Nez Perce encampment. We're planning on coming over."

"All right!" you say to yourself. "There's still some chance of salvaging this vacation."

THE END

It takes a lot of talking, but finally you and Tina convince the others to hang around with instruments ready. They were right; you find it is an awkward position. There you are, standing around, in the way, hoping someone has a disaster like a heart attack or something.

Then it happens. Not a heart attack, but the sax player for another group is so drunk he can't make a toot. That group has to cut out one of their songs, and it leaves room for the Idaho Blue Mountain Stampede to do one number.

Quickly you all set up, and before you know it the tape begins to roll. In three minutes and twenty-four seconds it's all over. But it did sound good. The gang's happy they waited around.

Mike comes over to thank you for convincing them to stay. "We didn't have much time on the air, but who knows? It might be just the break we need. Anyway," he continues, "the guy over at the lodge likes us so much he wants us to play over there all of next week. Can you help us out a little longer, kid?"

"Can I?" you hear yourself saying. "Of course I can!"

"A summer vacation of hiking in the woods, and playing the drums," you say to yourself. "I must have died: I'm in heaven."

THE END

You quickly explain the situation to the officer. Your detailed description of the pickup and Julie's account of the robbers' clothes give the officer positive identification. "It sounds like those boys who broke into Deer Lodge last week," he says. "Listen, you two walk straight back to the bank and stay there until another officer arrives. He'll take down your story. And besides, this gal's mother is about to die of fright. I'll radio back that you're both OK. Then I've got to head through the woods here. There's a trail or two those old boys don't know about. I think I can stop them before they get to the highway."

The streets of West Yellowstone are mostly deserted as you go back into town. As you round the corner you notice a huge crowd in front of the bank.

When the two of you walk up, someone shouts, "Here they come! Here they come!" Then the whole crowd turns and there is thunderous applause. Everyone's cheering for you and Julie. She rushes into her mother's arms while a couple of strong men hoist you to their shoulders. You realize you're a celebrity.

Two hours later, after you give your story to the other officer, your dad grabs you by the arm. "Come on, superstar. You've got to get back to camp and help with dinner."

"Rats!" you say to yourself. "I'll bet James Bond and Wonder Woman never have to do dishes."

THE END

You're sad to see the group go. They provided your life with twenty-four of its most exciting hours.

"Sure, I missed the excitement in West Yellowstone, and even the president. But for a little while I was a professional musician," you say to yourself, "and I liked it!"

This is one dream you're not going to let evaporate. It didn't work out today, but someday it will happen. You make that pledge to yourself as you beat out the group's theme song on a nearby pine trunk.

THE END

The man in the Bermuda shorts gathers up the papers and heads out the door of the ranger station.

"Hey, where are you going?" the ranger asks. "Aren't you going to wait for Professor Way?"

"Tell him to come up to Great Falls sometime. I think I can make him a deal," the man says. "Here's my card."

You look at the card on the counter as the man drives north in his travel home. It reads, "Honest Andy's Antiques, 329 Timberline Drive, Great Falls, Montana."

"Nice work, kid." The ranger looks at you in disgust.

You walk back to camp with five hundred dollars in your pocket. That's more money than you've ever had.

"Not bad for one day's work," you say to yourself. "So how come I feel so rotten about it all?"

THE END

But you forget about the campsite mix-up, what with all the excitement. You go to bed early and can't get to sleep for thinking about being a drummer on tv. Finally you doze.

About 2:00 A.M. you wake up to a big commotion. You hear your uncle arguing with someone down the drive. Then your dad is up, and a sleepy-looking ranger appears. "The reserved campground!" you remember.

You run up to them and confess your lie about the campsites. Your uncle is disgusted with you. The ranger is mad. Your dad is furious. You have to tell them about the tv special, which you were hoping to surprise them with.

Your dad is adamant. "You are NOT going to play any drums on tv. Now get back to bed. I'll take care of this in the morning."

All your dreams crushed, you drag on back to your tent.

The next morning you have to break the news to Tina. Without a drummer, the Idaho Blue Mountain Stampede has to cancel their appearance on tv, and by noon they move on. Your uncle and family finally move into a campsite after spending an expensive night in a motel in West Yellowstone.

Your whole family wants to go down to the Fourth of July Celebration, but you decide to stay in camp. For the rest of the evening you lie on your sleeping bag, beating out a tune on the tent pole, and dreaming about what could have been.

THE END

"Listen, kid," the man says, "don't go away mad. So, we made a mistake about your friend. It's just that, as a rule, you can't trust those Indians. Now why don't you wait and get your picture taken for the paper? I think the bank might even have a little reward for your heroism."

"I'm not staying in this crowd," you tell him.

"Why not?" He actually sounds surprised.

"Because I don't trust them," you say as you walk away. You hope you'll be able to see Windy before you have to leave to go back to camp.

THE END

All that day your nervousness builds. As you sit behind the drums that evening, before the concert begins, you continue to pray for God's help. The camera crew lets you know that it's five minutes till you're on.

"Hey, everyone," Tina quiets the group. "Before we go up there, I'd like to have this kid pray for us. Listen up, you guys; we need it."

You take a deep breath and lead in prayer. A couple in the group snicker, but not Tina. Your group's part of the concert goes really well. Everyone seems to enjoy the music, and you don't make too many mistakes.

Afterwards, Mike and the bass guitar player head on off to talk to some record company executive, but Tina stays around to chat.

"Listen, I really appreciated that prayer," she says. "You know, I'm beginning to think there's something to this Christianity thing. I wish I knew more."

You invite her over to your family's campfire that night, and she spends half the night talking to you and your folks. Finally you doze off.

You can barely hear your dad as he leads you over to your tent. But as he closes the tent flap, you remember him saying, "What happened around the campfire was a lot more important than the concert."

You wonder what he meant, but only for a moment. Then you're fast asleep.

THE END

It's a huge picture of you and Buck. He's holding you close on his horse, and your eyes are open wide in real terror. How embarrassing.

"The boss says he wants to make sure you sign a contract to be in my next picture before you all leave the park," Buck says. "Maybe you and your folks could come on down to the set later this afternoon."

After Buck leaves, Carrie suddenly cries out, "But I didn't get his autograph!"

"Don't worry, ma'am," you tell her, lowering your voice in an imitation of Buck's drawl. "I'll give you my autograph instead."

You have to dive into your tent to avoid the wrathful barrage of well-thrown pinecones.

THE END

Soon you find yourself hiking back down the trail, with three armed gunmen right behind. One pushes you ahead of him, with your arm twisted behind your back.

Rounding a bend in the little dusty road, you all hear commotion in the trees. Straining their eyes to see, the bank robbers view a terrifying sight.

But it doesn't scare you a bit. There in the woods, mounted on horseback with rifles and shotguns drawn, are close to one hundred of Windy's relatives. Many, like your friend, are dressed in ancient costumes.

"I—I don't believe it," one of the thieves stammers. "Captured by Indians. Things like this aren't supposed to happen anymore."

You use the distraction to pull away from the robber and run over to Windy and SlamDunk. "Boy, am I glad to see you!" you say.

With guns confiscated and hands tied, the crooks are marched back to town in front of the Indian posse. They are led right over to the deputy sheriff. Then the Indians return to their encampment.

After talking to your folks, Windy's granddad convinces them to let you stay with Windy and his family for the night. That's when your adventure really begins. There, around the campfire, in recognition of your bravery and friendship with Windy, you are made an honorary member of the Nez Perce tribe.

THE END

But you are only halfway through the stagecoach window when the gunman grabs your feet and pulls you back inside. Thrown to the floorboard, with a heavy foot pushed against your back, you have no choice but to wait it out.

Turn to page 98.

You walk over to the tunnel exit, and Henry continues the conversation. "Well, we couldn't just keep quiet our whole lives. So the Lord provided us with different sanctuaries where it's perfectly allowable for us to talk. This valley is one of them."

"You mean there are more places like this one?" you ask.

"Of course! Now, run along. Maybe we'll meet again," Henry concludes.

"But, Henry, aren't you afraid I'll bring a lot of folks back here and expose your little valley?" you say as you start your muddy crawl through the tunnel.

"Not a bit. You'll never find it again once I cover the tunnel entrance," he responds.

On the far side of the tunnel you call back to Henry. "But what if I tell everybody about the fact that beavers can talk? Won't that jeopardize your position?"

"I'm not worried about that, either." His voice echoes over to you. "How many humans would believe a kid's story about talking animals?" Then Henry waddles out of sight.

As you walk on back to camp, you realize that Henry was right. In fact, that night at the family campfire, you show your great pictures of the hidden valley but don't bother mentioning talking beavers.

"No reason to get the twins laughing at me," you say to yourself. "Besides, I don't know if I even believe it myself."

THE END

"It's gold!" he shouts.

"It is?" you respond.

"Kid, we struck it rich. This old mine will be worth millions. And it was right beneath my feet all the time! We'll be millionaires, you and me!" He is almost dancing in a limping sort of way as he hobbles out the mine entrance.

"What do you mean 'we'?" you question. "It's the park's property."

"Nosiree. Pappy wouldn't let them have this part. It's forty acres that they could never get. I got clear title to it, and the mineral rights, too. And you are my new partner. Whoopee!" the old man shouts.

"Er, why me?" you ask.

"'Cause if you hadn't found me, and risked your neck to save me, and dug down under that shaft floor, that gold would still be hidden. No sir, we are fifty-fifty partners. Agreed?" He holds out his hand.

You hesitate for a minute, and then shake.

"The first item of business is to get this sample to the Assay Office in Butte," he says.

"The first item of business," you correct him, "is to get you patched up at a hospital."

"You're right, pardner." The old man smiles.

As you help him down the trail, you still can't believe your good fortune. "I hiked into the woods with only sixty-five cents in my pocket, and I'm leaving as a millionaire," you muse. "But I guess that's the way things happen in the wild West!"

THE END